This Book Belongs To

Pam Atwood
6 Country Lane
Eliot, Maine 03903

0-590-32571-X © 1982 Scholastic Inc.

THE CASTLE OF THE RED GORILLAS

WOLFGANG ECKE

Illustrations by Rolf Rettich

Translated from the German
by Stella and Vernon Humphries

Prentice-Hall, Inc.
Englewood Cliffs, N. J.

First American edition published 1983
by Prentice-Hall, Inc.
Englewood Cliffs, N. J.
First published in Great Britain 1983
by Methuen Children's Books Ltd
11 New Fetter Lane, London EC4P 4EE
Originally published in West Germany
by Otto Maier Verlag Ravensburg
in volumes entitled:
Das Schloss der roten Affen, Der Mann in Schwarz,
Das Gesicht an der Scheibe, Solo für Melodica,
Das Haus der 99 Geister, Schach bei Vollmund and
Der unsichtbare Zeuge
Copyright © 1971, 1972, 1974, 1976 and
1977 Otto Maier Verlag Ravensburg
This English translation copyright © 1983
Methuen Children's Books Ltd
Printed in Great Britain by
Butler & Tanner Ltd, Frome and London

Library of Congress Cataloging in Publication Data

Ecke, Wolfgang, 1927–
    The castle of the red gorillas.

    Translation of: Das Schloss der roten Affen.
    Summary: A collection of nineteen mysteries set in
Europe and the United States with solutions to be provided by the reader based on clues in the text. Includes
a section with solutions, explanations, and indica-
tions of degree of difficulty for each story.
    [1. Mystery and detective stories. 2. Literary
recreations] I. Rettich, Rolf, ill. II. Title.
PZ7.E1975Cas   1983   [Fic]   82-23122
ISBN 0-13-120360-6

CONTENTS

★	easy
★★	quite difficult
★★★	difficult

THE CASTLE OF THE RED GORILLAS

Some of the leading citizens of the French town of St. Lermain used to meet every Friday evening at the Black Rose Hotel for a drink and a chat. They did so as usual on May 12 last year, a date none of them was likely to forget in a hurry.

Around the table on that memorable night were Gustave Lerron, the pharmacist; Michel Jonas, the mayor; the police chief, Victor Collet; the owner of the supermarket, Robert Roche; and an insurance agent, Marc Loire. The headmaster of the boys' school, Charles Lupont, joined them later.

They had been talking quietly for about half an hour when Lerron, the pharmacist, tapped his glass for silence. "Gentlemen! If no one has any objection, I'd like to suggest a way of making our weekly gatherings more interesting." His lively eyes darted around, eager to see what the others had to say.

Robert Roche was the first to reply. "I must say I don't find these meetings of ours too dull, Gustave. But if you've had an idea, let's hear it. Tell us what it is, and as good democrats we'll vote on it."

Everyone laughed and seemed to agree with Roche.

Lerron cleared his throat. "I've been thinking that it might be amusing if, week by week, we took turns telling a story," he began. "Anything would do—something that had happened to the speaker, say, or an incident told to him by someone else. What do you all think?"

"Hm," grunted Collet, the police chief.

"I've no objection...." mumbled the mayor.

Marc Loire, however, a man with plenty to say for himself, grinned slyly. "You know what's behind all this, don't you?" he chuckled. "Gustave's heard some tale that he's dying to tell us. It's only to justify himself that he wants us all to follow suit." He raised his glass and took a sip. "If you want my opinion, I'd say Charles should begin. After all, as a schoolmaster he's paid to tell the children fairy tales."

The mayor, however, sided with Lerron. "I see no reason why Gustave shouldn't kick off. I'm all for it."

"So am I," said Robert Roche.

Collet too nodded enthusiastically.

Gustave Lerron clapped his hands together, pleased at the outcome. "You're outvoted, Marc," he declared with a broad smile. "And as you're always telling us how brave and enterprising you are, I'm going to tell you a tale that will make even your hair stand on end."

Loire bristled. "You do exaggerate sometimes, Gustave," he said with an impatient wave of his hand. "But in one sense you're quite right. I simply don't know what fear means. If you ask me, only stupid people are ever afraid."

Such a chorus of protests greeted these words that for a few moments no one could hear himself speak.

In the end it was Charles Lupont, the headmaster, who voiced the general opinion. "My dear Marc, fearlessness isn't always a sign of strength. Indeed, I'd go further. I believe there are times when every sensible person knows what it is to be afraid."

Marc was highly offended. "In other words, Charles, you consider me a fool?"

"I'm sure he meant nothing of the sort, Marc," said the mayor, trying to keep the peace. "You mustn't take Charles so literally. But no more arguing now. Let's hear this spine-chiller of Gustave's."

"Hear, hear!" said the others, and the pharmacist needed no more persuasion.

"You might call my story 'Alone with Seven Red Gorillas,'" he began.

"You call that a title?" objected Collet incredulously.

"What's wrong with it?" retorted Lerron. "One title's as good as another."

"I disagree with you, Victor," interrupted Roche, "I'd call it a very striking title."

The pharmacist thumped his fist on the table so hard that the glasses tinkled. "Shall I get on with it, or would you rather fight over the title?"

"We're all ears," the mayor assured Lerron, his eyes twinkling. He rearranged himself in his chair and adopted the pose of an eager listener, as if he were acting a part on the stage.

The others too turned to Lerron expectantly, curious to hear his tale.

"A traveling salesman from one of the big drug firms visits my shop regularly, and this adventure befell him the other day on his way from Paris to Orléans. His name is André Passou.

"He was driving along in his car when, without any warning, both his rear tires burst. It was only six kilometers to the next village, but he was carrying such a large quantity of medical supplies that he couldn't leave the car unattended. All he could do was sit there and wait for someone to pass that way.

"But everything seemed bewitched. The road was utterly deserted: not a car, not a cyclist, not even a pedestrian could be seen. Passou was almost in despair. At long last—and it was well after nightfall by now—an old woman appeared. She listened to André's tale of woe in stony silence, but in the end she promised she'd go and get help for the stranded traveler.

"Again Passou was alone, and time seemed to drag endlessly. Suddenly he jumped. In the distance he heard the unmistakable clip clop of horses' hoofs. And he was right. A wagon drawn by two horses came into view, driven by a man dressed all in black. The man explained that no one could fix the tires before morning, so he invited Passou to go with him to Castle Loupou, where he could spend the night.

"Although André had never heard of the place, he didn't hesitate. He and the wagoner transferred his belongings from the car to the cart, and only fifteen minutes later they passed through the castle gate. It closed behind them with a resounding clang.

"André could make out nothing of the castle except its outline. But soon they were indoors, and the man in black led him along echoing corridors, through vast halls and huge rooms which had only one thing in common: they were all empty. No furniture, no pictures, no carpets, nothing. At last they came face to face with a high wide door to which the wagoner put his ear, listening intently. As he did so, a piercing shriek was heard from within.

"André Passou gasped and felt his blood run cold. For his guide, however, the cry appeared to be a kind of signal. Without a word he thrust open the door and motioned to Passou to pass in front of him.

"Trembling, he staggered forward. He was so frightened, he could feel the sweat running down his back.

"He found himself in an enormous room in which hundreds of tallow candles were burning. In the middle was a table. It was lavishly set for two people, with fine china, antique silver cutlery, and rare cut glass, to say nothing of an abundance of mouth-watering dishes. Only one thing was missing—a host. Remembering the dreadful scream he had heard, André turned to his guide to beg him to explain the mystery . . . but the man had simply vanished.

"Passou was about to dash for the door when it reopened and a very old gentleman entered. His hair was snowy white and he looked as if he had stepped out of an old painting. 'My dear sir, please sit down and consider yourself my guest,' he said. Taking André gently but firmly by the arm, he led him to the table.

"Time and again, Passou tried to start a conversation, but he had no success. The only replies the old gentlemen offered were: 'Do have some caviar. . . . Why not try the lobster? . . . This breast of turkey is quite delicious, I assure you.'

"So passed the next half hour.

"Presently the white-haired gentleman opened

another bottle of wine. It was pinkish in color, the kind known as rosé. Good as it was, Passou thought it left a peculiar taste in his mouth. All at once his host's face seemed to crease into a mocking sneer. Passou, greatly puzzled, felt compelled to ask the man for some explanation. But try as he might, he found his teeth were so tightly clenched that he couldn't even open his mouth. Some strange change was taking place in his body. His legs and arms grew as heavy as lead, and the edges of the figure opposite blurred and wavered before his eyes, first slowly, then faster and faster....

"André Passou stared helplessly as, with a soft whinnying laugh, the old man rose to his feet and moved toward the door. He stood beside it and clapped his hands smartly, his fingers edging toward the light switch. Passou gazed at the door and the blood froze in his veins. Two gigantic gorillas, their shoulders hunched, were coming toward him, lurching from side to side. But it wasn't this alone that terrified him so. It was the yellow gleam of their protruding teeth and, worst of all, the fact that their shaggy fur was bright scarlet.

"'Can...can there be...such animals...as ...red...gorillas?' he asked himself, and it cost him a huge effort to form each word in his mind.

"In an instant, both animals were stooping over him, and for a few seconds he could smell their hot stinking breath. Imagine his horror when he saw the white-haired gentleman flick the switch and all around was pitch dark. Passou felt himself sinking to the ground, and he lost consciousness.

"When Passou awoke he was lying on a bed, but he couldn't make out where it stood for there was no vestige of light anywhere. It took him a minute to recall the sinister events so far. Then he cringed in terror. Something heavy had placed itself across his legs. Cautiously André raised the upper part of his body and his hand groped forward. But a moment later he plucked it back as abruptly as if he had thrust it into a naked flame. What he had felt was coarse animal fur. There was no mistake possible. One of the red gorillas was keeping watch over him.

"He lay still. His senses were sharpened, and he listened hard for any telltale sound. His ears registered a subdued whistling on his right, like a person breathing in his sleep. The same sound could be heard on the left as well. Could there be other victims besides himself?

" 'Hello!' he called softly into the darkness. 'Is there anyone here?'

"No answer.

" 'Hello!' he repeated, stretching out his left hand. The heavy breathing stopped abruptly and a shrill piercing yell rang through the darkness, echoing against the walls. Something gripped André's hand, and strong claws seemed to bore into the back of it. A hairy something glided across his face. The beat of his heart was almost too painful to bear.

"He jerked his hand free and, shaking all over, held his breath, expecting the brute to attack him. Yet nothing happened.

"After an hour or so, the animal lying across his legs changed its position. It slid down from the bed, and André heard the dull thud as the heavy body landed on the ground and the tap of its paws against what could only be a stone floor. Its self-satisfied grunts made Passou shudder.

"It was then that his eye caught sight of a small

patch of light on a wall. It must be a window, so André knew that day was breaking. After another twenty minutes he found he could make out a few more details. But they did nothing to encourage him. His bed stood in a very large room. And around it lay seven full-grown gorillas, all seven with identical bright scarlet fur.

"Ten minutes later still, André figured out that his room must be at ground level. He distinctly recognized the castle wall through the window, as well as the narrow iron gate through which he had come the night before. He also saw the trunk of a tree.

"André eyed the gorillas. They appeared to be fast asleep. Cautiously he drew up his legs. With even greater care, he swung them over the edge of the bed until he could feel the floor firmly beneath his feet. Oh, no! A spring creaked! Passou stopped dead. But the beasts must have been sleeping more soundly than he had thought. He judged the distance from the bed to the window to be between twelve and fifteen meters.

"Everything seemed to go smoothly. He was no more than three paces from the window when one of the scarlet apes gave a loud howl. As if at a word of command, the other six gorillas jumped up and joined in the infernal hullabaloo, which echoed round and round the room.

"Half crazed with fear, Passou bounded to the window and stretched out his hand to open it. But

it had no handle and needed a special key to open it. He turned around, cornered. He was so paralyzed with fear that instead of a cry for help, only a strangled gurgle escaped from his throat.

"Rearing to its full height, the largest ape was

only a few meters away from him. The other six, not much slower, were now closing in on him in a half circle—noiseless, unhurried, step by step. . . .

"The leader drew itself up, ready to pounce, when a brusque order rang through the room like a whiplash. Framed in the doorway stood the wagoner who had driven André to the castle the previous evening. In a matter of seconds, the room except for André and the bed was quite empty. . . .

"Had it been real, or nothing but a devilish nightmare of his imagination?

"When Passou reached the drive in front of the building, he saw his own car waiting there for him. The tires had been fixed, and the man in black was placing Passou's cases beside it.

"At the same time, the white-haired gentleman appeared at the door and walked over to André.

" 'My dear sir,' he said, 'I know you won't be pleased to see me again, and I'm extremely sorry for causing you such distress. At the same time, I should like to thank you in the name of science for having helped us in our research into human behavior under stress. As compensation for the high degree of fear you have suffered, allow me to offer you a fee of two thousand francs.' And he handed him an envelope.

"André Passou took the money without hesitation. As he drove away, his eyes wandered upward to the window on the second floor behind which, only minutes before, he had been alone—at the mercy of seven scarlet gorillas."

Gustave Lerron glanced around the table, "Yes, gentlemen, that's my story. I hope it didn't bore any of you."

For a while, there was complete silence. Lupont, the headmaster, was the first to speak. "In my opinion, such experiments are extremely sinister," he said gravely. "But I can't for the life of me see why the gorillas had to be bright red. I've never in all my born days heard of scarlet gorillas."

"Scientists often have the weirdest ideas," said the mayor. "But I must say I thought it was very decent of them to compensate the man so handsomely for what he'd suffered."

Gustave Lerron turned to Marc Loire. "And what has our hero to say to the story? How would you have behaved?" he asked, his eyes sparkling with irony.

"Your drug salesman seems to be very timid," replied Loire scornfully. "I dare say he'd have been just as scared if he'd been left alone with seven sparrows."

Lerron smiled charmingly. "That's exactly what I hoped you'd say, Marc. In fact, I happened to mention you to Passou, and I told him that you said you were never frightened, no matter what happened."

Loire nodded, a bit nervously. "At least I'd have earned my two thousand francs without making such a song and dance about it."

"I mentioned that to Passou as well. And he in turn got in touch at once with Professor Mendelle—he's the white-haired gentleman—and now the professor is eagerly looking forward to your active cooperation."

The deathly hush around the table lasted for several moments.

"What do you mean by my active cooperation?" inquired Marc Loire huskily.

"Simply this. Professor Mendelle is coming here to St. Lermain tomorrow morning to take you back to Castle Loupou with him. And the day after tomorrow, you'll be two thousand francs richer!"

The color drained from Marc's face and he threw up his hands helplessly. "I . . . I . . . I'm so . . . so sorry," he stammered. "I've just remembered, I have to . . . to . . . um . . . leave town in a hurry. In fact, I must be off right away. I qu . . . quite forgot I have to pack. I must go immediately!"

Loire scurried off in such haste that he left his hat behind.

Gustave Lerron took a deep breath. "At last!" he sighed, smiling to himself. "I've finally called his bluff and shown the braggart what fear is. And I don't mind telling you, it's a very satisfactory feeling."

Lupont leaned forward, his eyes wide with surprise. "Do you mean to say it wasn't true, Gustave?

That the whole thing was pure invention?" he asked incredulously.

"Of course it was," nodded the unrepentant Lerron. "As you said yourself only a moment ago, who ever heard of scarlet gorillas?"

"A thrilling tale, "said Collet, the police chief, who had spoken little so far, "and you told it splendidly, Gustave. But speaking as someone whose working life involves listening carefully to other people, I think you must be more careful next time. If Marc had paid more attention, he couldn't have helped noticing that you made two important mistakes."

"Did I?" Lerron was genuinely astonished.

"Yes, indeed, although they didn't have anything to do with the gorillas as such, nor with the car breakdown. Think it over."

Lerron took his words to heart. "So I will. And in future I'll make sure there are no police officers present when I have a story to tell!"

What were the two mistakes spotted by the police chief?

HAPPY EASTER!

The people of Oslo were most surprised to see snow again on Easter Sunday. For weeks spring had been in the air. The city's streets and squares had been free of ice and slush, the crocuses in the parks were in full flower. And then this!

The snow started falling about mid-morning and it didn't stop for the rest of the day. By the time Easter Monday dawned, the Norwegian capital lay under a blanket of snow which was growing thicker by the hour.

Detective Inspector Laurenz from the Oslo Crime Squad was far from pleased to be told that there was a Mr. Arne Nilsson to see him. The time was 10:30 A.M. "Why couldn't he have come in an hour and a half," grumbled Sven Laurenz to himself. He had been on duty since the early hours, and at twelve noon his colleague, Matt Osgard, would have arrived to take over from him.

And so Arne Nilsson found a not very friendly reception at police headquarters. He was too excited to notice, though. "I've been burgled!" he declared.

Sven Laurenz pointed to a chair. "Please sit down," he said. "First let me have your name and your occupation, and then tell me what's been stolen."

"My name is Arne Nilsson, and I'm a partner in the antique shop, Bjorn and Nilsson," he snorted angrily. "When I arrived at our business premises this morning..."

"But it's Easter Monday," Laurenz interrupted him. "Do you always go to your shop on public holidays?"

"Yes, and on Sundays too. I'm a busy man. As I was saying, I went to the shop as usual, and when I arrived I nearly had a heart attack." For a moment, he looked as if he might very well collapse, but he quickly recovered. "Three valuable pieces of sculpture are missing, as well as a unique diamond-studded snuffbox and a carved box of solid gold cutlery with place settings for twenty-four people. They've all vanished."

"And how did the thieves get in?" asked Laurenz, making a few notes.

"That's the whole point, Inspector," replied Mr. Nilsson, eyeing the ceiling with a strange look on his face. "No lock was forced, no windows were broken."

"I see from your expression that there's someone you suspect."

"Yes," hissed the antique dealer, his eyes glittering. "I suspect my partner, Knut Bjorn. He's a frivolous playboy who never has a penny to call his own. And do you know why?"

Laurenz shook his head.

"Because he gambles. Yes, Inspector, he gambles, and I for one never trust a gambler."

It was plain that Nilsson didn't think much of his partner. But was it simply on account of the man's gambling?

"What does he say about the burglary?" asked the inspector.

"Nothing, and for one very good reason. I haven't been able to ask him. I've tried to phone him at least twenty times, but there's no reply from his house."

Laurenz looked at his watch. Just his luck! He'd have to investigate this case after all. The devil alone knew when he'd get home. "I'll have one of my men take your complete statement," he said flatly. "Meanwhile, I'll go and see your partner before I go to the shop. What's his address?"

It was precisely 11:45 A.M. when Detective Inspector Laurenz reached Mr. Knut Bjorn's house in a suburb of Oslo. He rang the bell, and Bjorn himself answered the door. Bjorn was in pajamas. He seemed genuinely shocked to hear about the burglary.

He told the inspector that he had been fast asleep until the doorbell woke him up. And he also stated that he hadn't left the house since Saturday night. "I'd better get dressed and go to the shop with you," he said. "Can you give me a lift?"

Laurenz nodded. "Certainly."

"I have a car, of course," Knut continued, "but I've no car keys at the moment. I'll have to wait for the thaw before I can get them back."

"Why is that?"

"I was careless enough to drop them in the snow somewhere between the garage and the front door, and so far I haven't been able to find them. My wife has a second set, but she's out of town and won't be back until next week."

At the front door, Knut turned around to face the police officer.

"I wouldn't be surprised to find that Nilsson 'arranged' this burglary to put the blame on me," he said softly. "He can't understand why I like to take a little chance now and again. He's convinced that one of these days I'll gamble away the entire business. He doesn't trust me an inch."

It was almost 1 P.M. when the three men met in the antique shop—Arne Nilsson, Knut Bjorn, and Detective Inspector Laurenz. So far, Laurenz hadn't been able to establish whether or not the theft had actually taken place. But one thing he knew for certain. One of the two partners had told him a lie.

The question is: Who was the liar—Nilsson or Bjorn?

DINNER AT THE ZANZIBAR

With a sigh, the private detective Olaf Kellborn
eased himself out of his armchair, gave the television screen one last look, and went to answer the
door.

"Yes? What can I do for you?" he asked the man
there, who was fidgeting nervously with his hat.

"My name is Paul Oxter. I'd like a word with Mr.
Kellborn."

The detective motioned to him to come inside.
"It's always a pleasure to have visitors after ten
o'clock at night," he said rather sarcastically.

The caller seemed most apologetic. "I know it's
late, but you're the only person who can help me."

"I doubt that," said Kellborn drily. "There are
dozens of private eyes here in Stockholm who'd be
happy to chase even green and yellow ants for you if

you offer them enough money. But step inside and tell me what's worrying you, Mr. Oxter."

It was almost two minutes before Mr. Oxter could collect himself and start telling his story. But he had a good listener in Stockholm's finest private detective. "I ought to tell you first that I'm the catering manager at the Millberg factory half a kilometer down the road from here. More than four thousand people work there, and I'm also responsible for the cafeterias at two other factories. Every Friday evening, between six and seven, the managers of these cafeterias bring me the week's takings. They did so as usual yesterday—it was Friday, you remember—and I locked up the money in the safe, exactly as I always do."

Kellborn interrupted his visitor. "Do you live on the premises?"

"Yes and no. That is, I have a company apartment inside the factory, but there's a private entrance to it from Kolborg Street. My wife happens to be away just now—she's staying with her sister in Goteborg. This means that I usually eat out in the evening. So I left my apartment at eight o'clock last night, and I went into town for dinner at the Zanzibar Hotel."

"Phew! You certainly do yourself proud!" whistled Kellborn. "The food's fantastic. I go there myself now and then—when I can afford it. But with their prices, that's not very often." He paused a moment and then continued, "But isn't the Zanzibar somewhat out of your way? It must be an awkward journey for you."

"It's not too bad," replied Paul. "It takes me half an hour by car. After all, if you want a decent meal you make the effort."

"True enough," nodded Kellborn. "But I didn't mean to interrupt you. Please go on."

Again Oxter found difficulty in speaking, but after a while he pulled himself together and went on with his tale. "It's part of my routine to walk through the factory every night to make sure everything is in order. When I got back from the Zanzibar last night, I did exactly that. Everything seemed all right until I reached my office, and there I was absolutely stunned. Someone had broken into the safe."

Kellborn sat in silence for a moment. Then he asked, "Do you remember what time it was when you found the safe rifled?"

"Yes," replied Oxter immediately. "It was exactly 9:15. I remember looking at the clock, because I was about to call the police...."

The detective sat up abruptly. "Well? Why didn't you?"

Paul Oxter swallowed hard. He seemed very upset. "Because ... because ... it would all have come out into the open. You see, I'd forgotten to lock the office door! Yes, Mr. Kellborn, I'd simply forgotten to lock up. It's never happened before." At this point

Oxter paused and took a folded sheet of paper from his pocket. "I've made a list of possible suspects, people who know the layout and who would also have known there were almost forty thousand kronor in the safe."

Olaf Kellborn cast his eyes down the list of names. "Are you absolutely certain that the circumstances are exactly as you've described them, Mr. Oxter?" he asked searchingly.

The catering manager placed his hand on his heart. "Yes, yes, I'm quite certain," he replied excitedly. "The times, the names written here are all correct. But . . . but who are you telephoning?"

"Inspector Orldag at police headquarters," answered Kellborn with a smile. "He'll call me all kinds of names, but late as it is he'll come out here if I ask him to. And he'll tear your make-believe alibi to shreds, Mr. Oxter. I have a feeling that somehow or other the missing forty thousand kronor have found their way into your pocket. . . . Take it easy now, Mr. Oxter. The inspector won't be long."

What made the detective realize that the catering manager had told him a pack of lies?

A RED-HOT TIP

Eddie Smedley—nicknamed Sandy, no one knew why—sat in his favorite pub, The Blue Parrot, staring gloomily into his half-empty glass of beer. He cheered up in a twinkling, though, when an old friend came in and sat down beside him.

"Man alive!" exclaimed Sandy. "I never expected to see you so soon, Ollie. I thought you got two years!"

Oliver Hall nodded. "That's right, two years it was. But they knocked off a few months for good conduct. You know how it is. You pipe down, say 'Yes, sir' and 'Please, sir,' and then they let you out early for being a good boy."

The barman put a pint of beer in front of him. Ollie put it to his lips and he didn't set it down again until he could see the bottom of the glass.

"What are you doing now?" asked Sandy.

Ollie lowered his voice. "I've got a red-hot tip, Sandy. Lots of cash and easy stuff to unload. Feel like giving it a try?"

Sandy was too suspicious to hide his doubts. "Why don't you do the job yourself?"

"Can't. The fuzz are keeping an eye on me."

Sandy thought it over. "What's it worth?"

"All in all, ten thousand, I'd say. Six for you and four for me."

Sandy shook his head. "Seven for me, three for you."

Ollie Hall signaled to the barman. "Forget it, Sandy," he whispered. "I'll find someone who'll do it for six. I've got too much at stake to let it go for less."

Sandy made up his mind. "Okay, Ollie. Seeing as it's you, and you're just out of jail. How, when, and where?"

Hall leaned closer to Sandy. "Tonight. Take the bus as far as Simbrook, to the new houses they're building in King Henry Avenue. They're still paving the road and there's no street lighting yet. Most of the houses aren't quite finished, but one row of four is already occupied. Number twenty-four belongs to a chap named Mellor. He's away on vacation and he won't be back till tomorrow. You can't force the front door—there's a special security lock. But if you stand on a few bricks, you can easily cut a hole in the kitchen window. Mellor keeps his cash and other valuables in an old carved chest in the dining room."

"In the dining room?" echoed Sandy. "You must be joking."

"No, I'm not. This Mellor thinks he's clever, and I've heard him myself telling everyone within earshot that no burglar would ever look for cash there. He's too smart for his own good, if you ask me. What do you think?"

Sandy nodded. He agreed with Ollie, but he still wanted to be sure that there were no snags. "And it's really foolproof, is it?" he persisted.

Ollie sounded quite offended. "I wouldn't pull your leg, Sandy, not with four thou at stake. Here, pal, you've got an hour to spare. Time for another one. Cheers!"

In fact, they found time for another three pints of beer. And between The Blue Parrot and the bus stop, Sandy managed to pass four more pubs and have a drink at each of them. Now he was in the right mood.

He took the bus to Simbrook, got out at the right stop, and with light springy steps made his way to King Henry Avenue. The new development was still under construction, exactly as Ollie had said, and he had no trouble discovering the row of four completed houses.

As he approached his goal, Number 26 King Henry, he started humming softly. By placing three large bricks one on top of the other, he found he was at exactly the right height to cut a neat circle in the kitchen window, using the glass cutter he always carried with him. He pushed in the large disc without bothering to be quiet. Still

humming merrily, he reached through the hole and opened the window from the inside. He was still humming as he climbed into the kitchen.

A few moments later he was feeling his way along the hall and groping for the light switch. Suddenly the whole place lit up as if of its own accord.

On the landing stood a man, and he was pointing a shotgun at Sandy. "What do you think you're doing?" he shouted in a very angry voice.

Sandy stared as if he had seen a ghost. "I ... I ... thought you weren't coming home till ... " Muttering to himself, Sandy backed into the kitchen as the man advanced on him down the stairs.

"You can tell that to the police when they arrive," barked the man with the gun. "Sit down over there." He pushed a kitchen stool toward the puzzled Sandy. "The sergeant said he'd be here immediately."

Sandy collapsed on the stool, crestfallen. "Where did I go wrong?" he mumbled over and over again. "That's what I'd like to know...."

Where had *Sandy gone wrong? What was his mistake?*

A ROAD ACCIDENT

It was April 27, 1978.

The clock in the church tower was striking ten when the accident happened in Byron Street. Two meters from a pedestrian crossing, an elderly lady was hit by a car and thrown to the ground. As usual on such occasions, the statements of the shocked eyewitnesses were wildly exaggerated and one contradicted the other. Some spoke of the reckless driving of the man at the wheel, while others declared that the victim had shown complete disregard for her own safety.

An ambulance took the injured woman to the nearest hospital, and the driver had to go with the police officer who had been summoned to the scene. He did so under protest, maintaining he was innocent. When they reached the nearby police station, the unfortunate man was taken to the duty room.

"Please sit down and show me your driver's license," said Sergeant Kelly, pushing a chair toward the pale and trembling figure.

The man sat down heavily and mopped his forehead with his handkerchief.

"It really wasn't my fault," he insisted. "The woman stepped straight into the road without looking left or right."

The police sergeant nodded and looked at the man's driver's license. "We'll make a note of everything you say," he promised. "You're Mr. Hulbert, I see."

"Yes."

"Your full name, please."

"Peter Frederick Hulbert. I'm a traveling salesman for Greene's, the knitwear manufacturer, and I've never had an accident before."

Kelly nodded. "And the date of birth here, March 19, 1950, is correct?"

"Yes, that's right."

"What about the address, Eighteen Kennedy Avenue? You're still there, I take it?"

"Yes, I haven't moved. . . . But I sounded my horn, Officer. I don't like doing that—it often frightens people, don't you think? But there must be witnesses who heard it."

Large beads of sweat kept forming on Hulbert's forehead so that he was constantly dabbing them away. He seemed to be exceptionally upset. His eyes looked feverish and his voice was hoarse as he assured Sergeant Kelly, "This is the first time in my life that I've had anything to do with the police. I hope you've taken the addresses of the passers-by."

The sergeant waved his notebook. "It's all down

here," he answered. "Names, addresses, and statements."

"Surely they all said I'm completely innocent. It isn't always the driver's fault. There are careless pedestrians, too."

"There are indeed," agreed the policeman. "And if they break the law, they can be punished as well, don't you worry."

Hulbert shrugged his shoulders helplessly.

The officer pointed to the door. "Will you kindly wait outside for a few minutes? I want to telephone the hospital."

"Yes, yes, of course. Do ask how the poor woman is. I'm very sorry, although it was no fault of mine. Perhaps she can be asked to confirm my innocence, if she's well enough to talk."

Hulbert tottered from the room, his knees trembling. The sergeant's glance followed him. As soon as the door was closed, Kelly picked up the phone. "Kelly here," he said. "Get me Greene Brothers, knitwear manufacturers. . . . No, I don't know their number, but it'll be in the book."

In less than two minutes he was speaking to the company's personnel officer. Kelly's approach was calm and matter-of-fact. "It's nothing serious, Mr. Shotter. A salesman of yours, a Mr. Hulbert, has been involved in an accident. I only want to ask you how long he's been with your company."

"One moment, please, while I look up his file."

Papers rustled at the other end of the line. Then Mr. Shotter's voice could be heard again. "He's been on our payroll for seventeen years."

"And may I ask if you're satisfied with his work?"

"What an odd question! It's hardly likely we'd have employed him for seventeen years if we weren't satisfied. In fact, Mr. Hulbert is our best and most hard-working salesman, and we'd be very sorry to lose him."

"Thank you, sir. That's all I want to know."

Kelly's next call was to the hospital. "Put me through to the emergency room, please."

This second conversation lasted four minutes. Then Peter Hulbert was summoned back to the duty room.

"How is the lady, Officer?"

"There's no cause for alarm, Mr. Hulbert. It's a compound fracture, but the doctor thinks she'll be on her feet again in about six weeks."

"Thank goodness for that!" said Mr. Hulbert, again wiping his brow.

"And now we come to the second point," the sergeant continued.

Hulbert was completely taken aback. "The second point? What else can there be? Is there some new evidence against me?"

Sergeant Kelly shook his head. "Not on the reckless driving charge, if that's what you mean."

Peter Hulbert stared. The color had drained

from his face. "But . . . what else can it possibly be?" He could barely speak.

"We'll have to go to another part of the building, I'm afraid. You'll soon find out what's wrong."

"But where? I don't understand a word you're saying, Officer."

Kelly paused before answering. "We're going to run an identification check, Mr. Hulbert."

Hulbert's face turned gray. His arms drooped helplessly. "Identification check?" he whispered, scarcely audible.

"Yes. I regret to say that there's something very fishy about the driver's license in your possession. Unless I'm very much mistaken, it looks as if it's been forged."

Why did Sergeant Kelly suspect that Hulbert's license had been tampered with? What was wrong with it?

THE DISAPPEARING VOLKSWAGEN

The large public parking garage outside the Town Hall had room for a hundred and eighty vehicles. It was divided into Blocks A, B, C, and D, each manned by a full-time attendant. Since they shared the work equally, each of the four attendants had forty-five parking spaces to look after.

The entrances were separate from the exits. The parking fee was calculated according to the length of time the car would be parked, and it was paid when the car arrived.

It was 7:45 A.M. precisely when a gray Volkswagen drove into Block B. The car was the first to arrive at that block; in fact, the whole garage was almost empty.

A man with a big bushy beard and sunglasses got out of the Volkswagen. He wore a checked peaked cap and a light raincoat. He locked his car carefully and beckoned to the Block B attendant, Alfred Whicker.

"What's happened?" asked the customer. "Why aren't there any cars here?"

Alfred Whicker grinned. "In half an hour there won't be a single space left. You're lucky you could get here so early. How long will you be leaving the car for, sir?"

The Volkswagen driver wasn't quite sure. "I won't be back before eleven o'clock," he said vaguely.

So Alfred Whicker told him how much it would be for four hours' parking; the driver paid and got an official receipt.

8:30 A.M. As the attendant had predicted, the Town Hall Parking Garage was absolutely full. To the right of the Volkswagen was parked a dark red Mercedes sports car. Ten minutes earlier, a white Ford had pulled into the space to the left.

Not far away, a man had his eyes glued on the area concerned. He watched closely everything that was going on in the neighborhood of the Volkswagen. He wore a brown suede jacket and a deerstalker hat. A curved pipe was clenched firmly between his teeth. Only the most acute observer would have realized that this man in country clothes was in fact the very person who had left the gray Volkswagen, wearing a raincoat and a peaked cap.

8:40 A.M. This seemed to be the moment the man in the brown jacket was waiting for. While the attendant was busy taking money at the far end of Block B, he sprang into action. Swiftly, but without drawing attention to himself, he approached the gray Volkswagen.

Thirty seconds later the car drove off unnoticed, leaving by the usual exit.

And three minutes later still, Alfred Whicker motioned a bright yellow Toyota into the now empty space. It didn't worry him in the least that the Volkswagen had left so early. After all, the driver had paid in advance for a four-hour stay.

11:10 A.M. The man with the bushy beard, sunglasses, and light raincoat stormed toward Alfred Whicker. "What's happened to my car?" he yelled.

"The Volkswagen?" stuttered the attendant, staring at the space now taken by the yellow Toyota, and by this time, it so happened, flanked by another two cars of the same make.

The man in the raincoat seized Whicker by the lapels and shook him. "I hold you responsible!" he thundered. "There were valuable paintings in that

car, as well as two sculptures which are worth thousands!"

A passing policeman hurried to the scene. "What's going on here?" he demanded.

The bearded man released Whicker and turned to the policeman. His voice was so excited that he could hardly get the words out. "This is supposed to be a supervised garage, "he fumed. "If the attendants do their job, how is it possible for a car to be stolen from here?"

The policeman couldn't think of an immediate answer.

"Listen, Officer," continued the Volkswagen driver, waving his hands angrily. "I left my car here at a quarter to eight this morning. When I returned a minute ago, it had gone. Can't a man leave his car in an attended garage for three hours without someone stealing it? What are we paying for if the cars aren't safe here, that's what I want to know. They're taking our money on false pretenses!"

The man tugged at his beard while Alfred Whicker's hands grew damp with dismay. Meanwhile, the policeman tried to disperse the gathering crowd before addressing the irate driver. "Where exactly did you leave your car, sir?"

"In the space that yellow Toyota is in. The cars on either side of mine were a dark red Mercedes and a white Ford."

With a glance at the ever-increasing number of

inquisitive onlookers, the policeman said, "You'd better come with me to the police station. I'll have to take statements from you both."

Ten minutes later, at the station, the policeman began taking down the two differing statements.

All at once, Alfred Whicker sprang to his feet. Pointing to the Volkswagen driver, he shouted furiously, "I've got it now! This man's a liar!"

He seemed to have hit the nail right on the head, for as quick as a flash, the bearded man jumped up and disappeared through the door.

Alfred Whicker took a deep breath and plumped down on a chair. "Lucky I saw through him just in time!" he said with a sigh of satisfaction. "He tried to be too clever, and he overplayed his hand. If he hadn't made such a crucial mistake...."

What was the bearded man's mistake? Obviously he planned to claim his car had been stolen so he could recover the cost of the paintings and sculptures as well as the cost of the car itself. But what gave the game away?

FRONTIER INCIDENT

When did it happen? On December 2, 1981.
Where did it happen? At the customs checkpoint on the frontier between Austria and Germany.

There was hardly any traffic crossing from Austria into Germany on that December evening; in the last four hours, only three vehicles had gone through customs. It was very rare for things to be so slack. Not that the customs officials and frontier police were complaining. For several hours an icy wind had been blowing through the valley, and there was a nasty drizzle—the kind of light rain that changes to sleet from time to time.

This peaceful spell was not destined to last much longer.

At 23:10 hours the phone on Sergeant Siegel's desk rang. As he listened, the information he was given was so startling that he jumped up from his chair. But before he could ask any questions the caller had hung up.

The sergeant summoned the other officers together without delay. "I've just had an anonymous telephone call," he explained. "I was told that a car will be here quite soon, a Fiat with French license plates, and that hidden inside it are containers with ten kilograms of drugs. We've work to do, boys!"

The red alert was given. The frontier barrier was closed and every man on duty was ready.

The minutes ticked by slowly.

All eyes were fixed on the Austrian stretch of the valley. It was a winding road with a long succession of S-bends right up to the frontier post. At last, in the far distance, they made out a pair of headlights; close behind them was another pair. There was no doubt about it. Two cars would soon reach the checkpoint.

Every now and then they both disappeared from sight, only to reemerge.

Finally, the first car arrived and drew up in front of the customs barrier. Sergeant Siegel gave a cry—it was a black Fiat! And it had French license plates.

The Fiat was beckoned into a side bay just as the second car halted. This was a dark green Opel with a German license plate. The initial letter was M, which meant that it was registered in Munich. The driver was asked the usual: Anything to declare? And when he answered No, he and his passenger

were allowed through into Germany. The officials were interested only in the Fiat.

Meanwhile, this French-registered car had been taken to the garage, where two specialists immediately went to work to check it thoroughly. The French couple who owned the car protested loud and long, but to no avail. Half an hour passed, but nothing was found.

Toward half-past midnight, two more cars pulled up, again heading for Germany. The first one was Dutch, a Saab registered in Amsterdam. The other was a Triumph sports car, a brown one, and it carried Austrian license plates. After they'd answered routine questions, both drivers were allowed to proceed.

It was almost 3:00 A.M. before the disappointed customs officers, shaking their heads and muttering, began putting the Fiat together again. They had found nothing whatever.

They knew now that someone had played a hoax on them.

But was that the end of the story? No!

In the early hours of that morning, a car skidded off the road into a tree about fifty kilometers into Germany. The occupants were taken to the hospital. When the vehicle had been towed to a garage, several kilograms of hashish were found hidden inside the car.

An on-the-spot investigation showed that the car had crossed into Germany from Austria. And it was also confirmed that it had passed through customs after the Fiat had been stopped.

The anonymous accusation against the French-registered car turned out to be a false one. It had clearly been intended to throw the customs men off the real scent, and to keep them extremely busy at a crucial moment.

In which car were the dope smugglers: the Saab, the Opel, or the Triumph?

A DANGEROUS GAME

Alma Honeysuckle, short, stout, and fifty-three years of age, sat sobbing on the couch in her living room. It was in a terrible state, and she had no need to spell things out to Sergeant Popper who had been summoned to the scene. The place had been ransacked. Drawers had been emptied onto the floor, pictures torn from the walls, plants tipped out on the carpet. Old letters, books, and the contents of a sewing-box were scattered everywhere.

The same chaos could be seen in the other three rooms. It looked as if a hurricane had raced through the small house.

Sergeant Popper patted Mrs. Honeysuckle's arm soothingly. "There now, madam, try and calm yourself. We need a clear description of the intruders. The sooner we circulate it, the better chance our men will have of catching the villains. Please tell me what they looked like."

With a great effort, Mrs. Honeysuckle pulled her-self together. "They were between twenty and twenty-five, I'd say," she began, dabbing the tears from her face. "One wore a faded denim jacket and blue jeans. The other had dark trousers, a bright yel-low shirt, and a corduroy jacket. Oh yes, and he wore glasses too."

"Did they speak with any particular accent?"

"I really couldn't say. I expect I was too scared to take it in if they did. But one thing I'm sure about. When they'd finished, they drove off in a battered old Mini, a light-blue one."

"That's most helpful, Mrs. Honeysuckle." Ser-geant Popper seemed very pleased with the infor-mation. His colleague, who had been taking notes throughout, dashed off in a great hurry to circulate the *Wanted* notice.

Popper meanwhile tried to establish more de-tails. "You said you'd been to the bank to draw out 500 pounds, and that you came straight home after-wards."

Mrs. Honeysuckle nodded. "I only called in at the bakery on the way. You know how things are. With all that cash in my handbag, I didn't want to be out too long, not with all the muggings you hear about."

"And you didn't notice the two men in the street?"

"No, not till they burst into the house. It was ex-

actly twelve o'clock when I came in. The clock was striking as I took off my coat and put the money away in the green vase standing on the bookcase. I've hidden money in that vase for the last twenty-five years, and it's always been all right till now. Then I went back to the kitchen to make myself some tea. I was about to fill the kettle when I heard a sound like a key dropping on the floor. I turned around and there they were, coming straight for me. 'Where's the money?' they shouted. Before I could scream, they stuffed a dish towel into my mouth and tied me to a kitchen chair. Then they tied the chair to a radiator pipe."

Alma Honeysuckle began sobbing again. "I . . . I could hear them in the living room. They were throwing everything about. I was praying hard that they wouldn't look in the vase. How could I tell my husband that the 500 pounds had gone?

"But they found the money in the end. It was two hours before I could free myself and phone you."

Sergeant Popper didn't interrupt. He inspected the ransacked rooms once more, a knowing smile on his lips.

Half an hour later, the second police officer returned. "Bill and Henry have combed the neighborhood," he said, shaking his head, "but no one has seen either the two men or a battered light-blue Mini."

"I'm not surprised," said Sergeant Popper, getting to his feet. "Mrs. Honeysuckle is a charming lady, but she's also a very good storyteller and a most convincing actress."

The woman in question stared. "What . . . what are you saying?" she stammered, turning as white as a ghost.

"What I'm saying is that you've made it all up. You tried to throw dust in our eyes, but unfortunately for you, you tripped yourself up."

Alma Honeysuckle swallowed hard, but said nothing.

"I dare say it's true that you drew out the money—the bank will tell us that—but only you know why. Probably you want to buy something your husband won't approve of, and so you invented the two burglars."

"B . . . but you can't p . . . prove it!"

The officer shook his head. "There's no need to, Mrs. Honeysuckle. You've kindly supplied the proof yourself. Telling lies isn't as easy as some people think. You've been playing a very dangerous game, though, misleading the police."

And this time, Alma Honeysuckle's tears were real.

This is a difficult case. To solve it we need to know what was the crucial mistake made by Mrs. Honeysuckle in her statement to the police.

THE STOLEN TUNE

James Gilbert from Washington, D.C., was a successful stamp dealer. His hobby was playing the guitar, which he did very well. He also wrote songs when he was in the right mood.

One September evening he was in Chicago attending a stamp exhibition. After dinner at his hotel he went for a stroll around the block.

Suddenly he stopped dead and listened hard. Over the noise of the traffic he could hear a stereo, and the tune was strangely familiar. It sent shivers down his spine. It took him a minute to be a hundred percent sure, but then he knew. The group was playing a song he had written, one that had never to his knowledge been recorded. There was no doubt about it. Someone had stolen his tune.

James Gilbert did not hesitate.

He located the apartment from which the music came. Its owner was only too pleased to show him the record in question. From the sleeve he got all the details he needed about the group, the record company, the publisher, and the supposed composer.

It was the composer's name that gave him a shock. It appeared to be a certain Francis Hilton. And that happened to be the name of the manager of Gilbert's Washington stamp shop, although the man was always known as Frank.

As chance would have it, the music publishers concerned had their headquarters in Chicago. So the next day, as early as he could, Gilbert called at their offices. This time, it was the company's turn to be surprised. They showed Gilbert the manuscript, written in his own hand, but signed as if it were the original work of Francis Hilton. He was shown the contract too; this also bore the same signature.

Although Gilbert was seething with rage, he kept his head. Business must come first, so he continued his trip; he went on from Chicago to Detroit and Boston before returning home at the end of the week.

When he was back in his Washington office, he sent for his business manager. The following conversation took place:

Gilbert: I'd no idea you were a musician, Frank.
Hilton: Excuse me? I'm not a musician.

Gilbert: I'd call anyone who writes songs a musician, wouldn't you? Especially if they've been published and recorded.

Hilton: But I've never written a song in my life!

Gilbert: You never said a truer word. You only stole a song of mine and passed it off as your own work! That's known as piracy among musicians. But in your particular case, as you sold it for publication, it's stealing, Frank, just plain theft!

At this point Hilton turned deathly pale and groped for a chair.

Hilton: Only Bobby Berg could have played such a trick on me. (Berg was the firm's accountant.)

Gilbert: You're crazy! Why should Bobby do such a thing?

Hilton: He hates me. He'd stop at nothing to get me into trouble. He couldn't have guessed that you'd look up those publishers while you were in Chicago.

Gilbert: But it's your signature on the contract. I've seen it often enough to recognize it.

Hilton: He forged it.

James Gilbert paced up and down the room for a while. Then he sent Hilton away and a few minutes later rang for the accountant, Berg.

Gilbert: Did you know I'm interested in music?

Berg: Sure. You play the guitar. Everyone knows that.

Gilbert: And what do you play?

Berg: Nothing. I'm tone deaf.

Gilbert: Is it true that you can't stand the sight of Frank?

Berg: If you want the truth, yes.

Gilbert: A song I wrote has just been published and it's been issued under Frank's name. He's suggesting that *you* did it, to get him into trouble with me.

At this point Bobby Berg also turned deathly pale and groped for a chair.

Berg: He's a liar! First of all, I've no idea where you keep the songs you write. And secondly, I can't read music. I couldn't even have copied it properly. And I wouldn't have known if it were any good in the first place.

Gilbert: And you've never been in touch with any music publishers?

Berg: Never in my life. Besides, I'd have had to forge Hilton's signature, which is a criminal offense. I'd never risk that. You could go to prison for it.

Gilbert: Okay. You may go.

James Gilbert rested his chin on his hands and thought long and hard on what he had heard. After fifteen minutes' reflection, he believed he knew which one of the two men had stolen the song he had written.

The question is this: Who was guilty of stealing James Gilbert's tune, Hilton or Berg?

A MESSAGE IN CODE

The convict Hugh Wimpey, generally known as Fingers, was in a jolly and friendly mood on this particular day. He pushed the bin of dirty laundry past Prison Guard Hubbard with such enthusiasm that you'd have thought he'd been waiting all his life for such a job. And it was this unexpected gusto that made Hubbard begin to smell a rat.

Once his suspicions were aroused, he followed every movement the prisoner made out of the corner of his eye. It didn't escape his notice that as Wimpey delivered his load, he brushed against the van driver not once but twice. And each time it looked as though the encounter wasn't wholly accidental.

Twenty-five minutes later, Hubbard stood before the prison warden, Rupert Hunt, and handed his superior a note with an air of triumph.

"I've discovered this, sir. I found it among the laundry leaving the prison in the van."

"And who wrote it? One of our inmates, I suppose?" asked Warden Hunt, taking the note from Hubbard's hand.

"That's right, sir. It was Fingers ... I mean ... "— here Hubbard corrected himself quickly when he saw the warden's disapproval—"It was Number 192, Hugh Wimpey, in Block J. He intended to smuggle a message outside. I've already had a word on the quiet, you might say, with the driver. And he admits that he was expected to deliver it to Wimpey's brother, who lives in Dingley."

"Have you said anything to the prisoner?"

Hubbard shook his head and pointed to the note. "I wanted a word with you first, sir," he said, slightly embarrassed. "It's written in code, as you can see. I haven't been able to crack it. Perhaps we should call in an expert."

The governor smiled. "We don't want to make fools of ourselves, now do we, Hubbard? Take another look at it. I think you'll be able to solve Wimpey's secret code. He's only telling his brother the time and day he'll try to escape. I'm afraid we'll have to put a spoke in his wheel." And he handed the paper back to the guard. "Here you are. Read it again."

"All right. I'll have another try, if you like, sir," mumbled the guard sourly. He'd much rather have called in an expert. But he dutifully read the words again . . . and again . . . and again.

In fact, he had to read them many, many times. And it was only after the seventeenth try that a smile of satisfaction lit up his face. For the last time, he examined the text:

DAY	NEXT	FREEDOM	HAVE
READY	BEFORE	TWELVE	TWO
CAR	BID	WEEK	FOUR

"I've got it!" exclaimed Hubbard, beaming. "Yes, you're right, sir. It says everything—the exact time as well as the day. Amazing!"

And this explains why Fingers' attempt to escape from prison failed so sadly. He landed quite literally in Guard Hubbard's arms.

At what time and on which day did Prisoner 192 intend to escape?

SUPER SLEUTH, SWEDISH STYLE

Here is something a little different. This story was written by a teacher in a village school near Falun in Sweden. His students tried to find all the mistakes he planted in it. Try it yourself and see how many you can find!

Gunnar Falk was old and so hard of hearing that without a hearing-aid he was completely deaf. All the same, he was fitter than many a man half his age. For instance, every morning except on Sundays he used to walk the five kilometers that separated his house from the nearest village and then return on foot. That meant he was clocking up a steady seventy kilometers a week in all.

Mr. Falk had two passions in life. One was watching television; the other was reading and listening to detective stories. That one day he himself would be involved in a real "whodunit" was something he'd never expected to happen, not even in his wildest dreams.

It was a Friday.

It had been announced that that evening, Swedish television would be showing one of the best-known thrillers from the days of silent films. So Gunnar decided that instead of his usual daily walk into the village, he'd take the bus into town to have his hearing-aid repaired. When he got to the shop, he was terribly annoyed to discover that it would have to be sent away to the factory for repair. It wouldn't be ready for at least five days.

Well, it couldn't be helped. There was nothing for Gunnar to do except go home again without his hearing-aid.

So he was in a very bad temper when, in spite of everything, he sat down that evening in front of his television set to watch the film: *Murder on the Jumbo Jet*.

It was very exciting, and just as a man with a lisp was saying the words "I recognize you!" Gunnar's heart jumped. He distinctly heard the sound of someone trying to open his front door with a key. He leapt to his feet, tiptoed from the room, and flung open the front door.

A masked man was standing there, but he was so taken aback that he offered no resistance.

He allowed Gunnar to lock him in the kitchen. When the police arrived fifteen minutes later, they found the unsuccessful intruder sitting with his ear to the wall, listening spellbound to the film in the next room. The officers had trouble persuading him to leave the film and go with them to the waiting police car.

Well, Super Sleuths? That was the Swedish story, and it has several mistakes in it. How many of them can you find?

THE WIDOW FROM AUSTRALIA

It was June 20, 1978. That was the day when Jefferson Kirby, the chief cashier at the City Bank, Oxford, succeeded in robbing his employers of 300,000 pounds by means of a most cunning fraud. However, clever as he was, it took only ten days for the police net to close in on him. He was arrested and given a heavy sentence. But the money itself was never found.

Edinburgh, May 18, 1982.

The caller eyed the beautiful, expensively furnished room to which the housemaid had shown him with the liveliest interest. "I'll tell madam you're here," she said, blushing under the scrutiny of the lean young man's penetrating eyes.

Exactly five minutes later, Pamela Ferguson entered the room. She was twenty-nine years old, a pale beautiful woman. Her sad expression was only

emphasized by the cut of her elegant but plain black dress, set off by a valuable diamond brooch.

"You've come from an insurance company, I believe?"

The visitor bowed slightly. "I'm Arthur Robbins from the Silver Star Company in London," he introduced himself. Even as he spoke, it crossed his mind that he had in fact spent far less time in London recently than in Oxford.

"I can't remember asking your company to send me an agent," remarked Mrs. Ferguson. Her voice was charming.

"I'm sorry, but there must have been some misunderstanding." Again he gave a little bow. "I'm not an insurance agent. I'm the company's chief detective."

Mrs. Ferguson suddenly sat bolt upright, all attention and curiosity. But not a muscle twitched in her beautiful face as she pointed to an armchair. "Do sit down and tell me what I can do for you, Mr. . . . Mr. . . . ." She hesitated.

"Robbins," the detective reminded her. "Arthur Robbins."

He sat down, placed his fingertips together with studied care, and pursed his lips. "If I may, I'll run over the ground very briefly. You're Mrs. Pamela Ferguson; you arrived in this country from Sydney, Australia, seven months ago; and you've made your home here in Edinburgh. Your husband was Paul

Ferguson, a stock-breeder in Parramatta, who was killed in a road accident on August 26 last year." He looked at the lady innocently and asked, "Have I left out anything, Mrs. Ferguson?"

The woman dabbed the corner of her eye with a lace handkerchief and shook her head. Then, gazing hard at the detective, she said tearfully, "I think you owe me an explanation, Mr. Robbins."

He agreed courteously. "You mean that it's rather tactless to remind a young widow of recent unhappy events when she's trying to forget them by settling somewhere completely fresh?"

She nodded. "You've put it rather clumsily, but certainly that's how I feel."

"I should explain, madam, that the reason for my visit comes under three headings," he continued somewhat awkwardly. "So far, I've dealt with one. May I tell you about the second?" Without waiting for permission, he went on, "Almost four years ago, a certain Jefferson Kirby robbed the bank where he worked of 300,000 pounds. Although there was an army of policemen on his heels, he had the nerve to go straight to London to marry a certain Diana Balman. Just imagine, on that day of all days— first the robbery, then the wedding! A cool customer, this fellow Kirby, and a good organizer into the bargain, don't you agree? Of course he was caught, but. . ." Robbins paused, shook his head as if baffled, and then, staring fixedly at the pale Pamela

Ferguson, went on with his tale. "The case wasn't closed, however. Although Kirby was behind bars . . . sorry! I'm being tactless again. Although Kirby had been caught, the money and his young bride both vanished into thin air. Not a trace was left. Until today. . .

"But what happened next? Ah! That's the really exciting part of the story! The organizing genius Kirby got a sentence of ten years' imprisonment, but that was no use to the insurance company concerned, the Silver Star. Until, that is, my directors had a brainstorm." Here Robbins tapped his chest importantly. "They decided to put me on the job. I was relieved of all other duties, you understand, and told to devote my time to solving the mystery." Here he lowered his voice and his eyes flashed in triumph. "I'm ambitious, madam. I made it my business to clear up the case. I was determined to solve the problem of the vanished fortune and the missing Mrs. Kirby. Do you understand?"

There was an icy look in Pamela Ferguson's eyes. "Why are you telling me this?" she challenged Robbins. "Why should I allow you to ramble on with this idiotic story? Can you tell me that as well?"

"Indeed I can," replied Robbins promptly.

"I can hardly wait!" jeered the lady coolly.

"The answer is that you are the Diana Balman whom Kirby married on June 20, 1978."

The woman leaned forward, her lips quivering

and her voice far less sweet than before. "You must be out of your mind!" She fairly spat out the words. "You're raving mad. I was never in Oxford in my life, and I know nothing about this Mr. Kirby of yours, nor of the crime he committed. You said yourself that I came from Australia only seven months ago, didn't you?"

The detective didn't deny it. Instead he said, "That brings me to the third heading. It's taken me the best part of four years to track you down. My notes fill a hundred and eighty pages."

Pamela Ferguson waved his remarks aside. "I couldn't care less!" she retorted. "And now it's my turn to tell you something. If you don't leave this house immediately, I'll call the police."

Robbins smiled shrewdly. "I'm the only person investigating this case. No one else knows anything about it. For 100,000 pounds it could remain that way."

The widow took the receiver from the phone, then paused. "Ask for Inspector McPherson," grinned Robbins, trying to be helpful. "He's the man you want."

Pamela Ferguson did indeed ask for McPherson. Arthur Robbins had to give her credit for sheer nerve.

"Hello? Inspector McPherson? There's a madman here," she shrilled. "He's mixing me up with someone else. I need your help!"

Robbins took the receiver from her hand. "Okay, Jock. It's all right to come with the arrest warrant. It *is* Diana Kirby and the game's up. Yes, she gave herself away. I bet her husband will be furious when he finds out."

The London detective was silent, listening to the reply at the other end of the line. Then he replaced the receiver.

"By the way, madam, I have more bad news for you," he declared, and he sounded almost sincerely sorry. "You made a very foolish mistake when you bought that passport in Sydney. Mr. Ferguson's widow Pamela is seventy-two years old. Not that we need that information now.... Come on, cheer up! We all make mistakes, you know, even the cleverest of us. McPherson will be here any moment."

Pamela Ferguson, alias Diana Kirby, had indeed made a very serious mistake. You could say she gave herself away. What was it she said that made Arthur Robbins sure he had the right person?

THE BIRTHDAY PARTY

It was a fine evening in June. Nearly seventy guests had arrived at Michael Sylvester's house for the party. The large garden was festooned with twinkling lights, and a modern string quartet played dance music on the veranda.

The party was in honor of Michael's only daughter Gwendoline. She was just twenty-one.

At two o'clock in the morning, when the musicians were nearly ready to pack up and go home, Sylvester's friend Philip McKenzie led his host aside. "A terrible thing's happened, Michael. Mary's been robbed. Someone's rifled her handbag." Mary was Philip's wife.

Michael was appalled. And his horror only grew when during the next half hour it came to light that others too had had money stolen.

Mr. Sylvester quickly telephoned Detective Inspector Boult. His hoarse voice was so insistent that it took Boult less than fifteen minutes to arrive. He had three men with him.

"But I can't understand it," said Michael Sylvester. "I've known every single one of the people here for years."

"What about the waiters?" inquired Boult. "How many were there?"

"I had five waiters," answered Michael. "And I also hired the string quartet to play for us. But the musicians can be eliminated. They played all evening without a break, and they didn't leave the veranda once. Oh, there was one other person hired. A maid to be in attendance in the ladies' cloakroom."

The police officer thought things over before making up his mind. "You can tell the musicians they may go home, but I'd like everyone else to go into the house so that we can question them. Tell them that we're relying on their cooperation, and it's important for us to conduct a thorough investigation. I'm sure they'll understand. However, if a few of them are genuinely in a hurry to get away, my men will take their names and addresses and allow them to go. Of course, we may want to interrogate them later if that proves to be necessary."

Sylvester fluttered his hands in despair. "Do you think you'll catch the thief?" he asked.

"We can only try," answered Boult. "The culprit

or culprits may have had an accomplice who cleared off hours ago. But we must make a start somewhere."

By this time there was widespread alarm, and everyone started turning out pockets and handbags to discover exactly what was missing.

The interrogations began, conducted by Boult and one of his men. The other two policemen stood by the front door to check those who declared they couldn't stay any longer.

Half an hour later, the list of those who had left the house and the reasons they gave was presented to Detective Inspector Boult. Here it is:

Mr. Christopher Lee, jeweler, and his wife: their children were alone at home and they didn't want to be absent too long.

Jack Bateman, antique dealer: he had to catch a plane to New York at 4 o'clock that morning.

Mr. Michael Brown, banker, and his wife: the dog had been left in and they simply had to take it for a walk before they went to bed.

Ben Sole, trumpet player: the Inspector had already said that all the musicians could go home.

June Chester, no occupation: she was so upset that she had to go home and lie down.

Andrew Pickles, painter: he couldn't think of a good reason, after all, so he changed his mind and stayed. (Boult crossed his name out immediately.)

Mel Santantonio, sales representative: his wife,

who hadn't been able to come with him, expected him home by 3:30 at the latest.

Detective Inspector Boult read the list through twice before he looked up. The two constables were alarmed to see that he was scowling. He immediately went in search of Michael Sylvester, and his face showed clearly how annoyed he was. "I'm sorry I haven't got better news for you, sir, but my men have stupidly allowed the thief to leave the house. Don't worry, though. I promise you we'll catch him all right. Now that we know who he is, it's only a question of time. Good morning, sir."

Who is the villain, according to Detective Inspector Boult?

THE ROAD THROUGH RUSHTON FOREST

The shortest way from Dillon to Earlbrook was through Rushton Forest. You could save at least fifteen mintues if you took that road, but there was one disadvantage. It was in a very bad state and was full of potholes. It was little used except on Saturdays and Sundays. Then it was very busy with people out for the day, especially cyclists and hikers.

Late one Friday morning, Tony Masters, assistant to the head ranger, came out of a side path to cross the forest road. But the moment he reached it he braked hard and his moped came to an abrupt halt. Barely fifty meters away he saw a light gray car. And four paces from it lay a bicycle. Between the car and the bike was a man.

Masters knew who the man was, even though he was lying face down with his head turned away. He was Joe Walters, single, thirty-nine years old, and the accountant and chief cashier at the Earlbrook brick factory.

Masters guessed immediately what must have happened. Walters had clearly been mugged. The bloodstain on the back of his head left no room for doubt on that score. Besides, there was an empty money bag by his side, and on it was the name of the nearest bank.

The young forester called Walters' name twice. There was no reaction. So Masters jumped on his moped and rode as fast as the machine would carry him to the nearest forestry hut where he could find a telephone.

It was about 11 A.M. when Sergeant Collins and his experts arrived on the scene, together with an ambulance. Meanwhile, Walters had recovered consciousness. His face was twisted with pain as he told his story. He had drawn the weekly wages for the Earlbrook brick factory from the bank in Dillon, as he did every Friday. As he left the bank, he saw that someone had double parked so that his own car was hemmed in. As a result, he had had to wait a good half an hour until the other driver returned. It was to make up at least in part for this lost time that he had taken the shortcut through Rushton Forest. The workers at the brickyard expected to be paid by eleven o'clock every week. As for the attack itself, he made the following statement:

As I came around the bend I saw that the forest road was blocked by a cycle lying across it. I slowed down, stopped, and jumped out of the car to pull the bike out of the way. As I did so, I suddenly heard a noise behind me, but before I could so much as turn to discover what it was, I felt a tremendous blow on my head and I suppose it knocked me out completely.

Sergeant Collins stroked his chin. "Where exactly was the cash and how much was there?" he asked thoughtfully.

"I had 15,000 pounds with me, and it was in a bank money bag, which I had put inside my briefcase."

"And where was the briefcase?"

"On the front passenger seat."

Collins made some notes while Walters fingered the bandage on the back of his head.

"And you can't give us any description of the attacker or attackers?"

Walters shook his head. "All I saw was that the man wore a stocking mask and a pair of tan gloves, leather ones."

The sergeant nodded. The experts measuring

the various tracks had finished by this time and Collins told Walters, "You'd better come with me to headquarters and we'll get you to sign a formal statement."

Two hours later, as Joe Walters signed the document containing his account of the mugging, Collins eyed him with a wry smile. And when he spoke, his words were bleak. "We're keeping you in detention, Walters, at least for now. Once you confess where the money is and who your accomplice was, we can take it from there. In the meantime, the best thing you can do is to think over the ridiculous pack of lies you've been telling us."

What was the telltale flaw in Walters' story that told Sergeant Collins the mugging was a fake?

THE DOOR-TO-DOOR SALESMAN

May 22 was a date that Mrs. Lynch was likely to remember for a long time. The day began well enough. The twins, Simon and Caroline, were going on a school trip, which meant that they wouldn't be home for lunch. It was a good opportunity for Mrs. Lynch to have her hair done, so she made an appointment at the hairdresser's for 11:30 A.M.

Mrs. Lynch knew she would have to hurry if she was to get all the housework done in time. But before long, everything seemed to go wrong. She simply couldn't get on with all she had to do.

The first caller was Mrs. Allen, her next-door neighbor. Mrs. Allen was very upset as she explained that her married daughter, who lived fifty kilometers away, had been taken ill suddenly, and

Mrs. Allen simply had to go and see her. She'd be away for several days. If Mrs. Lynch would kindly look after Hoppy, the canary, and water the houseplants, she'd be very grateful. As she left, she pressed her front door key into Mrs. Lynch's hand.

Next the phone rang. It was Caroline. No, there was nothing wrong, but Caroline wanted to tell her mother how the school trip was going, and everything they had done so far.

At ten past ten the doorbell rang for the second time. A door-to-door salesman wanted to demonstrate the latest kitchen food processor.

At eleven o'clock another salesman stood on the doorstep. He tried to get Mrs. Lynch to buy one of his rugs.

And at twenty past eleven, when she already had her coat on, yet a third young man appeared, who wanted her to subscribe to some magazine or other.

At about three o'clock in the afternoon Mrs. Lynch returned home from the hairdresser's only to find that the house had been broken into. The burglars had taken all her jewelry, some cash, an expensive camera, as well as a valuable pair of binoculars.

Her neighbor's front door key had also disappeared. It turned out later that the thief must have known that Mrs. Allen was away, for he took the opportunity to go through all the drawers and cupboards next door as well. The only thing that had been overlooked was a coin collection, but that must have been pure chance.

When Sergeant Simpson was called to the house, he asked Mrs. Lynch to tell him in great detail what had happened that morning, and particularly to try and recall her conversations with the three door-to-door salesmen.

It came as a surprise to Mrs. Lynch to hear the officer's explanation. "I'm sure that one of the three was the intruder, and that he belongs to a gang. It seems likely that you yourself as good as let him in. Still, if you can give us a helpful description, I hope we'll soon catch him."

Here are extracts from the three conversations that took place that morning. The culprit is revealed quite clearly:

The food processor salesman:
"Good morning, madam, I'd like to demonstrate our brand new multi-purpose food
processor. No, no, it won't take a
minute. . . . But madam, there's plenty of
time before eleven thirty. It's only ten after
ten . . . I'm sure you'll never regret buying
one. . . . You can show it to your husband
later even if he isn't in now. By that time
you'll have discovered how useful it
is. . . . I'd be delighted to come back this
evening, then . . . Oh, well, if you're really
not interested. Too bad . . . In that case I'll
call on your neighbor. . . . She's not at
home, you say? . . . I see . . . for a few
days. . . . Well, I guess it isn't my lucky day!"

The carpet salesman:
"Look at the quality, madam, you don't get
a rug like this at such a bargain price anywhere in town. . . . It's a once in a lifetime
opportunity. . . . It's dirt cheap, and such a
beautiful design, you can't turn it
down. . . . Let me make a suggestion. Allow
me to put it down in your living room,
madam, and if you don't care for it then, I'll

roll it up and go.... Really, madam, your hairdresser won't run away, but if I go elsewhere and you hear that someone else has snapped it up, you'll regret it for years to come.... Oh, well, all I can say is that you're the loser, madam, I assure you."

The magazine salesman:
"May I ask you which magazines you subscribe to, madam?... No, I'm not being inquisitive, but there's no point in offering you those you read already... It won't take you a moment to see our range—fashion weeklies, illustrated monthlies... Would your husband be interested in our sports or auto magazines?... I could easily come back this evening if you prefer.... In that case I can only apologize for disturbing you. Good morning!"

Which of these three conversations suggest that the man might come back and burgle the two houses?

LOOKING FOR A SCAPEGOAT

For days now, John Lowe had felt exasperated whenever he caught sight of the deep scratch running from front to rear along the right-hand side of his brand new car.

He knew exactly how it had happened. He had parked in the big underground parking lot at the movie theater, and the fact that the damage was entirely his own fault galled him day after day. For John Lowe was the kind of person who always tries to put the blame on someone else.

That evening, though, there had been no one else involved when he'd grazed the side of the car against a steel barrier. And since it was all his own fault, he would have to pay for the repair. And that went against the grain with stingy Mr. Lowe.

Having thought about it for three days, he came to a particularly mean decision. He would find a

scapegoat, some totally innocent person whom he could accuse of having scratched his car.

John Lowe's first step was to look for a street that would serve his purpose. He found a one-way street named Vernon Terrace, a narrow thoroughfare where parking was allowed.

The next morning, a Thursday, he set out early to carry out his plan. He parked his car, then parked himself! That is, he hid behind a large bush and lay in wait for a suitable victim.

At 11:05 the moment arrived. A medium-sized delivery van turned into Vernon Terrace and Mr. Lowe wrote down its license number. Half an hour later, he entered the local police station, where an elderly sergeant asked him what he wanted. And John Lowe began his tale of woe.

"It was like this, officer. About nine o'clock this morning, I parked my car in Vernon Terrace. Then I did some shopping and I had to go to the bank. When I returned to get my car at 11:20, I found that a delivery van had scraped against it and made a deep scratch all along the right-hand side. It's a brand new Ford. I've only had it two weeks."

The sergeant was most sympathetic. "Bad driving manners!" he nodded, and he sounded really angry. "People dash off without a word for fear of raising their insurance rates. Were there any witnesses?"

Lowe shook his head. "No, unfortunately."

"I'm afraid it will be almost impossible to trace a van like that. You've no idea how many there are in a town like this."

John Lowe now played his trump card. He sprang to his feet, pulled a slip of paper out of his pocket, and flourished it in the sergeant's face.

"I was able to get his license number, though. Here it is!"

The police officer beamed. "Good. I'll get someone to check it on the computer and in a few minutes we'll know who owns the van."

He took the receiver off the hook and then suddenly replaced it. The friendly smile had gone and his eyes glared. "I see! You're lying! You're looking for a scapegoat, someone you can blame for the damage to your car which was probably caused by your own carelessness." With a menacing frown he eyed Mr. Lowe and paused a moment. Then he went on, "And trying to make a false claim to a police officer is an offense."

John Lowe, as white as a sheet and weak at the knees, sat down heavily....

By and large, this case is a clear one. What made the sergeant change his mind? How did he know that John Lowe's case wasn't genuine?

ADVENTURE ON THE ELEVENTH FLOOR

Tom Lipman replaced the receiver. He flopped down in the worn leather armchair beside his bed and started thinking.

One thing was clear. He couldn't do a job like that without help. He needed a partner.

He thought of all the crooks he knew, the big-time boys and the petty thieves. But the more he thought, the harder it became to make up his mind. It was far from easy to find the right accomplice. Certain risks would have to be taken which could not be ignored.

He was on the point of giving up the whole idea when a name suddenly occurred to him: Sam Lugg, known by his nickname Smoky Sam because he was never seen without a pipe in his mouth.

Five minutes later, Lipman was at the wheel of his ramshackle old Ford, driving toward Singlewood, where Lugg lived in a wooden house with a good-sized garden. But Lugg had another hobby besides gardening: He was a burglar.

Sam Lugg was sitting outside his house, deep in thought and chewing the stem of his curved pipe, when Lipman pulled up. Rumor had it that he never took his pipe out of his mouth, not even when he went to bed.

"Hello, Tommy," he greeted Lipman, the pipe firmly between his teeth.

"Hello, Sam!"

Lipman sat down near Sam and went straight to the point. "Are you still up to it, Sam?"

"Of course!"

"I've got three thousand to hand out."

"Difficult?"

"Not so much difficult as awkward."

Smoky Sam's face fell. He disliked anything that wasn't easy. His empty pipe bobbed up and down between his lips as he took another one from his pocket and set about filling it with slow, deliberate movements.

"Come on, Tommy. Out with it! What's the game?"

And Tom Lipman told him. "You know the Omeda Building on Victor Street? I thought you would. There's an art dealer on the top floor—

pictures and statues, that kind of thing. It's called Gallery Lacoste. Ever heard of it?"

Lugg shook his head. "Not my line."

Lipman continued, "They sell paintings, fancy china, that sort of stuff. My client wants us to steal a set of pictures for him. There are seven that go together."

"Are they big?" asked Lugg dubiously.

"No, quite small, about thirty centimeters square. No weight, not really."

"What's the security system?"

"There are two doors with burglar alarms that are connected to the police station. But we wouldn't use the doors. We'd go in through a window."

Smoky Sam shook his head. "I thought you said it's on the top floor."

"Right. The eleventh to be precise."

"Phew! What the devil..."

"We'd get in from the roof. Let down a rope ladder and open a window."

Lugg shook his head, mulling it over. "Eleventh floor!" he muttered. "Roof...rope ladder...I'm a burglar, not a circus performer! When's it supposed to take place?"

"Saturday night!" Lipman was getting impatient. "Well? Can I count on you? Or shall I find someone else?"

Again Lugg's pipe swayed slowly up and down.

"Oh, well, I can't afford to pass up three grand. I'll do it."

"Good! Pick me up at my house just before midnight."

It was first thing on Sunday morning, twenty past midnight to be exact, when Lipman and Lugg reached the Omeda Building on Victor Street.

For an expert like Sam, sixty seconds was enough to pick the lock of the door at the back of the building. Although no one lived there except an old caretaker in the basement, the intruders decided it was safer not to use the elevator. There were two hundred and forty-two steps to climb before they reached the iron door leading to the roof. Lugg managed to force this lock in record time; in fact, he needed only eighteen seconds.

At 00:49 they stepped out onto the flat roof of the tall structure. Sam had butterflies in his stomach as he saw the small moving lights of passing cars fifty meters below.

Lipman secured the rope ladder to a chimney stack and gave Lugg the signal to go first.

Pipe in mouth and lying on his stomach, Smoky Sam worked his way little by little over the edge of the roof until his feet found the top rung of the rope ladder. His face was pouring with sweat, he was so nervous. Two minutes later he found himself level with one of the large windows of Gallery Lacoste. At exactly 1 A.M., all was ready. By cutting a hole in the glass, he was able to reach the handle and open the window inward.

Smoky Sam was working his way over the windowsill into the gallery when Tom Lipman began the three-meter descent to join him.

Five past one.

Lipman and Lugg stood among glass cases, table displays of works of art, statues, and walls covered with paintings. Lipman shone his flashlight all around until the beam rested on a large oil painting entitled *The Glutton*. Beneath it were hung a set of seven much smaller pictures, the ones they were being paid to steal.

"There they are, Sam," whispered Lipman.

They worked in silence and by two o'clock, the pair of scoundrels, Lipman and Lugg, had left the Omeda Building, reversing the route they had used to enter it.

Monday, 9 A.M. Brian Lacoste was, as usual, the first to arrive at the art gallery. And, as usual, he went straight to his office to put down his briefcase and to change the calendar. And to switch off the burglar alarm.

Next, he walked across to the showroom. But the moment he opened the door he stopped dead. Seven lighter patches on the wall beneath the picture of the glutton indicated an unmistakable fact.

And the broken window took his breath away, although only for a moment.

Luckily, Brian Lacoste was not only an expert on works of art, he also knew correct police procedure. So he locked the showroom door and made straight for the telephone.

"I haven't been inside the room," he assured the policemen who arrived within ten minutes. He unlocked the door for them.

It was about one o'clock that afternoon when Lugg was arrested. Lipman was picked up about two hours later.

Lipman and Lugg had only their own carelessness to blame for the fact that the police found them so quickly. They themselves were kind enough to provide the one clue needed.

What was this clue?

A CASE FOR PERRY CLIFTON

It was Sunday.

Perry Clifton, the London store detective, sat in his Norwood apartment. One of his hobbies was mending watches and clocks, and he was busy tinkering with an old alarm clock when the doorbell rang.

Perry opened the door.

"My name is Mrs. Dawson," the caller said. "You *are* Mr. Clifton, aren't you?"

Clifton nodded. The short plump lady before him, with her jolly but shrewd face, struck him as a familiar figure.

"I live across the road."

"Of course!" Perry slapped his forehead. "I know you now. You're the lady from the laundramat! What can I do for you, Mrs. Dawson?"

The lady leaned forward and lowered her voice. "People say you're a detective. If it's true, there's

something I'd like to discuss with you," she whispered in her softest voice.

"Please come in then," said Clifton, motioning her indoors.

"Well," she began after a moment's hesitation, "my first idea was to go to the police, but my John—he's my husband—said they'd laugh at me. It was he who thought of coming to you instead. So here I am!" She underlined her last remark with a firm nod of her head.

Perry smiled gravely, trying to look as serious as his caller seemed to be. "As you say, here you are. Won't you tell me what it is that alarmed you and Mr. Dawson so much?"

"Of course, but I don't want you to think that my John's alarmed. Nothing rattles him," she insisted, determined to remove any misunderstanding. "He never gets excited! The other day when we were shopping, I missed my footing and fell full length in the street." Her eyes flashed and her voice grew louder. "And do you know what my John said?"

Perry shook his head politely.

"He said, 'That's all right, Mary, if you feel like lying down don't let me stop you! Stay where you are. I'll be back soon!' That's what he said, did John. And off he went to the newsstand, leaving me to pick myself up as best I could. That's my John for you. He works on the railway, an engine driver."

"Why didn't your John come with you now?" interrupted Perry Clifton in an attempt to stem the woman's flow of words.

"Oh, he couldn't do that. He's on the late shift today. On the line to Exeter, you know. . . . Now, what was I saying?" Mrs. Dawson tried hard to think, propping her head on her hand and frowning for all she was worth.

"You wanted my advice, Mrs. Dawson," said Perry patiently.

His visitor laughed, stretched out one hand, and

cried, "That's right!" Then moving her head closer to Perry's she again lowered her voice. "Just imagine," she began. "I was in the kitchen cooking the dinner when there was a sudden bang. Did you hear it?"

"When?"

"Earlier on, about twelve."

"Yes, I did. It was a supersonic fighter plane."

Again Mrs. Dawson's eyes flashed, this time with indignation. "There ought to be a law against it! I got such a fright that I dropped the butter dish in the pan of soup simmering on the stove. And when I finally managed to fish it out, there was a pigeon sitting on my kitchen table."

"Really? A pigeon?"

"Yes, Mr. Clifton, a carrier pigeon. My John noticed right away that there was a tiny capsule tied to its leg."

"Apparently the supersonic bang frightened it too, so that it took refuge through the nearest open window. Did you let it go again?"

"Yes, I did. But not before my John had had a look at the message it was carrying."

Mrs. Dawson's hand slipped into her handbag and, with the expression of an actress making a grand entrance, she held out a piece of paper to Perry Clifton. "My John copied it down, word for word."

Clifton felt a odd tingle down his spine as he

took the scrap of paper from the woman. The note read:

"Copenhagen, September 12

Dear Jan,

Arrived safely and got in touch with B. immediately. He thinks the Guilder notes have come out very well and will buy them from us for 10,000 pounds. I'm just off to Stockholm. All the best.

Piet"

Mrs. Dawson stood up, eyeing the detective expectantly. "Well? What do you say to that?"

Clifton's face looked serious. "You certainly had the right idea, Mrs. Dawson. It clearly refers to forged banknotes, Dutch ones."

"And what happens now?" she asked, her eyes gleaming with excitement.

"You'd better go home, and don't breathe a word about it to a soul. I'll see if I can sniff out this mysterious Jan."

"But I thought. . ." objected Mrs. Dawson.

Perry Clifton laid a gentle hand on the woman's shoulder. "Do you want to risk your life, Mrs. Dawson? These people will be ruthless if they're cornered. They're a law unto themselves. How would you like to find yourself kidnapped and locked in a cellar? You don't want your John to spend months and months looking for you, now do you?"

All at once, Mrs. Dawson was in a great hurry. And from his window Perry Clifton could see her glancing back anxiously over her shoulder as she made tracks for her safe little apartment above the laundramat.

Thirty-six hours later, Perry Clifton had solved the case. The man named Jan lived in an old house at the end of Bolton Street. From the sidewalk, Perry could see clearly the double entrance to the pigeon loft tucked away under the gable of the dingy gray house.

Shortly after six that evening, Detective Inspector Scott and two of his men arrived from Scotland Yard and stood in front of the house.

By twenty to seven, it was all over.

The Special Branch officers found printing-presses and forged notes in the cellar. All in all, they would have amounted to 50,000 pounds worth of currency if they had been genuine.

When the trial took place a few months later, Jan van Kampen, born in Amsterdam, could hardly believe that it was a pigeon that had cooked his goose!

The problem for you to solve is this: What was the country of origin of the pigeon in the case?

THE QUEEN OF PICKPOCKETS

Her name was Lena, Lena Lang, and she was considered the Queen of Pickpockets. Only once had she been caught, and that was when the victim whose wallet she had deftly extracted from an inner pocket turned out to be a member of the police force.

Lena's success was due to one particular skill. She was a master—or rather a mistress—in the art of disguise. Whether she dressed up as a beggar, as a smartly dressed socialite, as a priest, or as a post-man, her disguise was always foolproof. No one ever suspected that behind the costume lurked Lena, Queen of Pickpockets.

It was September 27, a memorable day as Lena Lang was to discover. During the past week she'd fixed her attention on the main railway station of a large

German town. For four days running she had been so successful that she decided to continue there for a fifth day, this same September 27.

What she did not know was that many of her thefts had been reported. As a result, a massive police presence had been arranged for that very day. No less than ten railway policemen, as well as fourteen regular officers in plain clothes, were dotted around the station, ready to pounce.

This September morning, Lena Lang had chosen to dress up as a man in Bavarian national costume—leather shorts, a deerstalker hat with a jaunty tuft from a goat's beard, and a knobbly walking stick. She stuck a bushy beard on her chin and she held a pipe in her mouth. The disguise was complete.

And then things happened.

She had "accidentally" bumped into a well-dressed gentleman, with the result that his bulging wallet was now in her possession. Suddenly Lena became aware of a pair of eyes boring into her back. She turned slightly and from the corner of her eye she picked out a harmless-looking man behind her, a quiet type of person in an ordinary gray suit. She strolled past him as if nothing were amiss. But she knew that he was following her.

It was then that Lena Lang made the mistake of her life.

To shake off her pursuer who, she suspected, had seen her stealing the money, she decided she would have to slip away somewhere safe. And where safer than the ladies' lavatory? Unfortunately for her, this only confirmed the suspicions of the plainclothes man in gray.

When she appeared at the lavatory exit about six minutes later, a pair of handcuffs was smartly clapped on her wrists.

Why was it a mistake for Lena Lang to try to hide where she did?

SOLUTIONS

The Castle of the Red Gorillas, page 5

1. According to the story, the room in which the meal was served had hundreds of tallow candles burning. Yet when the old gentleman switched off the light, everything was said to be in total darkness.
2. When it grew light the next day, André Passou figured out that the room where he had spent the night was on the ground floor. Yet as he was driving away he is said to have looked up to the room on the second floor where he had been left alone with the seven scarlet gorillas.

Happy Easter!, page 20

It was Knut Bjorn who hadn't told the truth. He said he hadn't left his house since Saturday evening. But if that were true, how could he have lost his car keys in the snow? It didn't start snowing until Easter Sunday!

Dinner at the Zanzibar, page 25

According to Oxter, he left his apartment for the Hotel Zanzibar at 8 P.M. and found the safe in his office had been broken into at 9:15. He also said that it took him half an hour to drive to the restaurant and, it's safe to assume, the same time to return—a total of one hour's traveling time.

In that case he had no more than a quarter of an hour to spare. But dining at an expensive place like the Zanzibar would have taken longer than that. Oxter's claim that he had ordered a meal, eaten it, and discovered the burglary within a mere fifteen minutes couldn't have been true.

A Red-Hot Tip, page 30

Our friend Sandy had had too much to drink. Instead of breaking into number twenty-four King Henry Avenue, where the owner was away, he had cut the kitchen window of number twenty-six, where the owner was very much at home!

A Road Accident, page 35

The accident occurred in April 1978. The date of birth shown on the driver's license was March 19, 1950, and Mr. Shotter of Greene Brothers said that Mr. Hulbert had been on their staff for seventeen years.

From 1950 to 1978 is twenty-eight years. If you take seventeen years from 1978, the result would be that Mr. Hulbert started work—and work that involved driving a car, what's more—in 1961, when he would have been only eleven years old!

The Disappearing Volkswagen, page 41

The driver of the Volkswagen claimed that he had been away from the garage for about three hours. How then could he have known that a red Mercedes and a white Ford had been parked on either side of his car, since both had long since left?

Frontier Incident, page 47

The drug smugglers were in the dark green Opel with the German (Munich) license plates. Only they could have known that there was a French-registered Fiat immediately ahead of them. And they were the only ones in a position to take advantage of the fact that the customs officers were concentrating all their attention on the suspect Fiat.

A Dangerous Game, page 51

The battered light-blue Mini was Alma's downfall. How could she have known how the burglars made their getaway, or what their car looked like, if she were tied to a chair, which in turn was tied to a radiator pipe, and it took her two hours to free herself?

The Stolen Tune, page 56

It was Frank Hilton, not Bobby Berg. James Gilbert's business trip had taken him to Detroit and Boston as well as Chicago. Only someone who had been in touch with the music publishers would have known for certain that their headquarters were in Chicago, and that that was where Gilbert would have gone to see them.

A Message in Code, page 62

If you want to know what Hugh Wimpey was trying to tell his brother about his planned escape, just read alternately one word from the beginning of the text and one word from the end. It reads as follows:

DAY	FOUR	NEXT	WEEK
FREEDOM	BID	HAVE	CAR
READY	TWO	BEFORE	TWELVE

Or, in plain language, he intended to escape the following Wednesday at 10 A.M.

Super Sleuth, Swedish Style, page 66

There were four mistakes in all:
1. Gunnar walked sixty kilometers a week, not seventy. He didn't go into the village on Sundays.

2. A silent film couldn't have had the title *Murder on the Jumbo Jet*. There were no jumbo jets in those days.
3. In a silent film, there couldn't have been a lisping voice nor could the intruder have listened spellbound to the film.
4. Gunnar had had to leave his hearing-aid in town for repair. Without it, according to the text, he was completely deaf. So he couldn't have heard the noise of someone trying to open the front door with a key.

The Widow from Australia, page 70

During the conversation between Arthur Robbins and the woman who called herself Pamela Ferguson, the detective did not mention Oxford, the place where Jefferson Kirby committed the bank theft. But when she was accused of being Diana Kirby and not an Australian widow, she protested that she had never been in Oxford in her life. She couldn't have admitted her guilt more plainly.

The Birthday Party, page 77

The most suspicious name on the list, according to Detective Inspector Boult, was that of Ben Sole, the trumpet player. Although he was a musician, he couldn't have been playing on the veranda all evening, as the music was provided by four string players and the trumpet is a wind instrument.

The Road Through Rushton Forest, page 82

Walters stated that he heard a noise when he got out of the car to clear the bicycle from the path, and that before he could even turn around, he received a blow on the head which knocked him out. In that case how could he declare that his attacker wore a stocking mask and tan leather gloves, if he hadn't had time to see who it was before he passed out?

The Door-to-Door Salesman, page 87

The first one, the food processor salesman, arouses the most suspicion. He was the only one who knew not only that Mrs. Lynch was going to have her hair done, but also that her neighbor's house was empty. She didn't mention this to either of the other two callers.

Looking for a Scapegoat, page 93

John Lowe had said that he found his car was damaged when he returned to Vernon Terrace at 11:20. The sergeant became suspicious when the man presented him with the license number of the van. If the damage had really been done in his absence, and there were no witnesses, how could he possibly have known the license number?

Adventure on the Eleventh Floor, page 97

Look again at the illustration. It can safely be assumed that the pipe on the table was not one of the art treasures on sale at the Gallery Lacoste! So having found it, the police knew at once that Smoky Sam was likely to be one of the culprits.

A Case for Perry Clifton, page 104

A carrier pigeon invariably returns to its own loft, so the answer must be England. Piet had sent the message by pigeon post, believing that this was the safest way of letting Jan know what had happened. But thanks to the Dawsons—and to Perry Clifton—he was very much mistaken.

The Queen of Pickpockets, page 110

Normally it wouldn't have been at all suspicious if a woman went into a ladies' lavatory at a railway station. However, in the heat of the moment Lena Lang forgot that she was convincingly dressed as a man. How could she fail to arouse suspicion?